Les Michailidis, I am forever grateful for your kindness.
I wish you a thousand happy birthdays!

Stay in touch at www.piccopuppy.com and @PiccoPuppy on Instagram and Facebook.

Picco Puppy books are available in personalized, bilingual, French, Spanish, Italian, German, Chinese, and Japanese editions. Visit www.piccopuppy.com for more information.

A special thanks to my wonderful team: Eugene Smolenceva (illustrator) and Brooke Vitale (editor).

Font Credits
Lost Brush by Stripes Studio
Marck Script by Denis Masharov
Cormorant Upright by Christian Thalmann
Century Schoolbook by Morris Fuller Benton
Copse by Dan Rhatigan
Josefin Sans by Santiago Orozco

First published in 2023 by Picco Puppy

Marketing Munch Pty Limited DBA Picco Puppy, PO Box 103, Killara, NSW 2071, Australia
Picco Puppy® is a registered trademark of Marketing Munch Pty Limited

A catalog record for this book is available from the National Library of Australia
ISBN 978-1-76133-451-1

I Wish You A Happy Birthday

MICHAEL WONG • EUGENE SMOLENCEVA

Lucy, once upon a time,
my every dream came true
when life gave me a precious gift:
the joy of loving you.

How much you've grown amazes me—
a real delight to see.
Lucy, I'll be proud of you,
whatever you will be.

Lucy, you're my everything;
you have my heart and soul.
The love I feel each day from you
has made me true and whole.

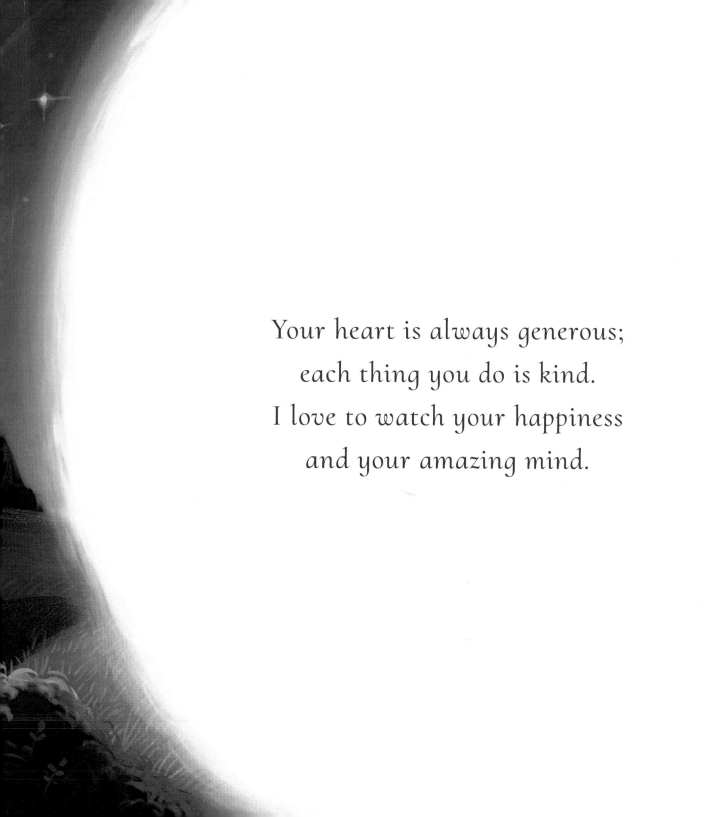

Your heart is always generous;
each thing you do is kind.
I love to watch your happiness
and your amazing mind.

With you, each moment's fabulous;
you brighten every day,
whether there's a clear blue sky
or one of cloudy gray.

Lucy, you're my miracle,
a brightly shining star.
I love you more than you can know,
and just the way you are.

I've never known a soul, my *Lucy*,
who's as unique as you.
I know there's nothing in this world
you cannot be or do.

How high you'll go is up to you,
no one can truly say.
I promise through the highs and lows
to be there all the way.

Whenever life has got you down
and you feel rather blue,
I'll wipe away your tears, my dear,
and hold and comfort you.

I love you more than all the stars
that fill the evening sky.
I love you so much that I sometimes
feel like I could fly.

Lucy, we will celebrate
this very special day.
I hope that you enjoy the treats
that soon will come your way.

May every wish you make come true
in this and every year.
I love you, and I wish for you ...

a happy birthday, dear!

Can You Spot the Famous People?

Lucy, no matter what obstacles you face, believe in yourself and all that you are—
just like these famous people did. Can you spot all five in the book?

Can you spot a young Robert Wadlow?

Robert Wadlow was born in 1918. He was the tallest person in recorded history, at a height of 8 feet 11.1 inches or 2.72 meters. Wadlow required leg braces to walk, but he never used a wheelchair.

Can you spot a young Claude Monet?

Claude Monet was born in 1840. He is a famous painter, best known as one of the founders of the Impressionist movement. Critics first said his paintings looked unfinished, but they later praised his work.

Can you spot a young Tom Whittaker?

Tom Whittaker was born in 1948. In 1998, he became the first person with a disability to climb Mount Everest, the world's tallest mountain. Whittaker's right foot was amputated following a car accident in 1979.

Can you spot a young Felix Baumgartner?

Felix Baumgartner was born in 1969. In 2012, he skydived from the edge of space at a height of 24 miles above the Earth's surface. Baumgartner became the first person to break the sound barrier (767 mph) in freefall.

Can you spot a young Mildred and Patty Hill?

Sisters Mildred and Patty Hill wrote the song "Good Morning to All" in 1893. Years later, the lyrics changed to "Happy Birthday to You." It is the most recognized song in the English language.

Can You Spot the Dogs?

There are twelve cute dogs in the book, *Lucy*. Can you spot them all?

Havanese

Irish Setter

Basenji

Coton de Tuléar

Siberian Husky

Belgian Malinois

Giant Schnauzer

Akita

Italian Greyhound

Bloodhound

Shetland Sheepdog

English Cocker Spaniel

Hi, it's Michael here, the book's author.

I hope you enjoyed the book. I'm also the author of *The Unconditional Love Series: I Wish You Happiness* and *I Will Always Be Proud of You*. I hope you collect them all.

As an appreciation for your kind support, claim your gift at www.piccopuppy.com/gift.

Michael Wong is an award-winning children's author. He is passionate about creating beautiful, empowering, diverse, and inclusive books for children. Michael lives with his wife and two children in Sydney, Australia.

Eugene Smolenceva is a creative artist with a passion for creating beautiful illustrations for children's books. Her illustrations are designed to evoke interest and positive emotions from both children and parents.

The Unconditional Love Series

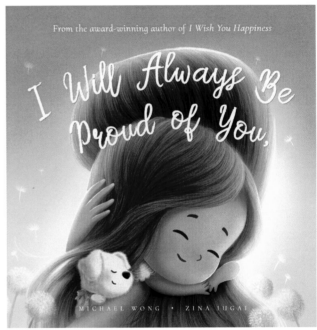

Available at PiccoPuppy.com,
Amazon, and all good bookstores.

Made in United States
North Haven, CT
02 July 2023